Keith Hatton

PROFESSOR PLUNDER'S
TIME MACHINE:
SEIZING CAESAR

Illustrated by St~~

CW00858212

To Svetlana,

"There's no limit to
your imagination!"

Keith Hatton

GINGER CAT TALES

Professor Plunder's Time Machine:
Seizing Caesar

Copyright © 2019 Keith Hatton
Text copyright © 2019 Keith Hatton
Illustrations copyright © 2019 Stewart Harris

First published in Great Britain 2019

All rights reserved. This book is sold subject to the condition that it shall not, by way of trade or otherwise, be lent, hired out or otherwise circulated without the publisher's prior consent in any form of binding or cover other than that which it is published and without similar condition, including the condition, being imposed upon the subsequent purchaser.

No part of this publication may be reproduced, stored in a retrieval system, or transmitted, in any form, or by any means, electronic, mechanical, photocopying, or recording or otherwise without the prior written permission of the publisher.

1 3 5 7 9 10 8 6 4 2

FIRST EDITION

ISBN 978-1-9164991-6-4

Printed in Great Britain November 2019

Special thanks to my family
for all their positive feedback and ideas.
Also, thanks to Miss Knight and Hardwick School
for their editing help.

Dedication

What would I do without my
best friend and wife, Emma? xx

INTRODUCING...

Professor Plunder

Ava

Clank

Darius

CONTENTS

CHAPTER 1:
Not Really a Morning Person

Professor Plunder was awoken by the hideous, piercing sound of his alarm. Loud and high-pitched was the only way to wake up this hard-of-hearing grouch. He didn't see this as a friendly wake-up call so – as he did every morning – he grasped the sledge hammer by his bed and swung it down with immense force onto the innocent alarm clock.

"Clank! Get online and order me another alarm clock!" yelled the professor, whilst wearily pushing himself off the bed and attaching his metallic peg-leg.

Within seconds, a speedy little robot came whizzing into the room, holding a trayful of breakfast in his two metal arms. He was the shape and size of a small, rectangular garbage can and lit up the room with the different LED lights, switches and gadgets all over his body. "Yes, Mr Plunder sir," replied the robot, as he nervously placed the tray on a side table.

"It's *Professor* Plunder, you great can of tuna! How many times do I have to tell you? One day I'll get around to fixing all of your glitches."

Clearly, the professor was not really a morning person.

In fact, he wasn't really an anything (or anyone) kind of person.

As Clank drew the enormous curtains, he revealed an even more enormous window, which unveiled a stupendous warehouse; as tall as a skyscraper and as wide as six football pitches. In front of them was a production line, busily churning out some nasty looking robot soldiers, who, when completed, stood in formation awaiting the professor's commands.

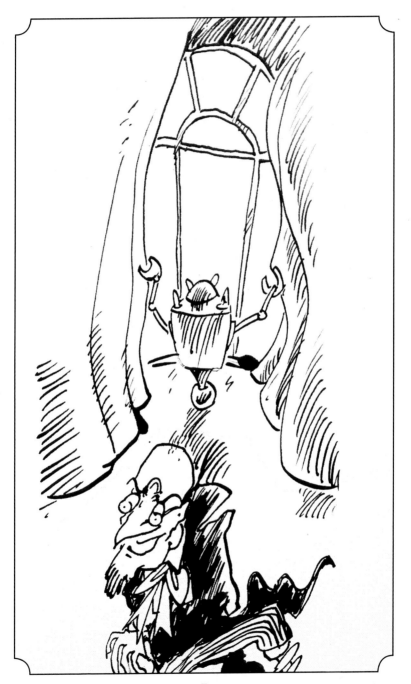

Clank glimpsed a large pile of broken robot servants in the corner of the warehouse. They had been discarded by the professor over the years and were a clear reminder to Clank to serve his master well or – as the professor liked to say – 'end up on the servant scrap heap.'

"Ah! My factory!" exclaimed Professor Plunder with a renewed skip in his step. "Another day, another attempt to conquer the world." He rubbed his hands together with glee then put on his black leather mad scientist coat and electromagnetic glasses, before making his way to the next room (ignoring the breakfast lovingly prepared for him by Clank).

"Clank! Get in here! I need to shout at someone!" Head bowed, Clank glumly followed the professor, accepting his fate.

In front of them was a very impressive-looking machine. The door was shaped like a diamond and the whole machine was completely transparent, with flashing buttons – as well as an electronic display screen – on the front door. On top of the device were two giant metal antennae, linked together by a severe, clearly powerful electric current. This machine meant business!

"What is wrong with this thing, Clank? I can't open the door!" said Professor Plunder aggressively, kicking the machine.

"That's the coffee machine, sir… I mean, Professor. Have you turned your glasses on this morning?"

"Of course I have. I'm not a buffoon!" he grumbled, whilst switching on his glasses and spinning around to look at the actual time machine.

"There you are my beauty."

Arms outstretched, he gave the machine a wet, toothless

kiss. "Are you ready for some more people stealing today?" he asked the inanimate object. "You were such a good girl yesterday, yes you were… who's a good girl? Hmmm…?"

Unable to cope with this putrid show of affection, Clank interrupted: "What about the prisoners Professor?"

"*Guests*, Clank. They are our guests, not prisoners."

The professor hobbled across the room and pushed a large red button on the wall. A panel slid open to reveal three humans; each with different confused, frozen expressions on their faces. They were kept inside glass cases (a bit like human-sized test tubes) and had all sorts of pipes attached to their hands, feet and mouths. All three of them had their eyes closed and looked like they were in one long, deep (wet) sleep.

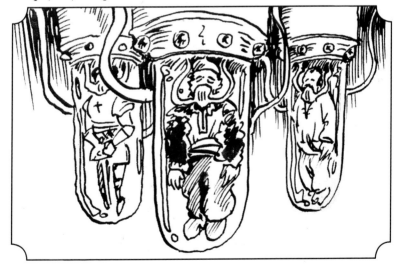

"Here they are!"

Professor Plunder pointed to the first container where a bearded, unusually-dressed man floated in a trance.

"William Shakespeare. The greatest and most famous writer of all time! How I love the characters he wrote about; Lady Macbeth, Richard III, Iago… to name but a few villains that I take inspiration from. When we wake him up, he'll be my chief speech writer, especially when I address the people of Earth for the first time! Ha ha, what fun!"

The professor turned his attention to a rather short, stocky (and very hairy) man who – even in his sleep – looked intensely angry and fierce.

"Attila the Hun. Or should I say 'the man who is soon to be in charge of my robot army'. In his time, he was feared by all his enemies and even chose to attack the great Roman Empire. A brave, fearless warrior and a lover of war; just what I'm looking for."

"Are you sure he won't mind that you kidnapped him and froze him in time?" piped in Clank.

"Oh, do be quiet you expired can of pickled peppers! He is an ambitious man and will of course be happy to assist me," responded Professor Plunder, with a slight quiver in his voice.

Changing the subject, the professor turned to a young lady, clad in armour but still hovering in her container. "Now, this is another legendary warrior to add to my army! Joan of Arc died far too young and had so much more to offer."

"Didn't she hear voices?" interrupted Clank.

"… And what's wrong with that? Anyway, she *actually* had visions and predicted events before they happened. She was powered by 'God' and I would like to take advantage of that."

"Fair enough," replied Clank, with a sigh.

Next to the three floating 'great people of history' were many more empty containers.

"Our work has only just begun, Clank. Now, ready the time machine. We're going on another plundering adventure!"

The professor made his way to the diamond-shaped door, nonchalantly typed '44BC Rome' onto the digital screen then stepped inside. Two mechanical arms dropped from the ceiling, helping him into a rather tight black suit before he sat down in a large metal chair, which was heavily bolted to the floor, and strapped himself in. Lastly, the mechanical arms placed thick protective glasses around his face and vanished back into the ceiling of the machine. Meanwhile, Clank zoomed around the room, pushing buttons and yanking levers before shooting inside next to Professor Plunder.

"We need someone to lead our special group of prisoners... I mean guests. I know just the man! Clank: I want a profile of Emperor and General Julius Caesar. Immediately. Come on!"

Like a mini-projector, a light began flickering in Clank's belly. A short presentation beamed out on the walls of the time machine, saying:

JULIUS CAESAR

Gaius Julius Caesar was a Roman dictator who lived from 100BC – **BC. He was a ruthless politician, as well as a skilled writer, speaker and army commander.

After a successful early career in the army, he became a member of a leadership group called 'The First ***********'. This included Caesar's close ally, *******, and a celebrated Roman commander called Pompey. The three of them ruled Rome (and its republic) together until Caesar defeated ****** during a civil war.

This meant that Caesar was now head of **** and made

himself 'sole ********'. In the year that he ruled, Caesar made many changes to the lives of ordinary Romans, especially to veterans of the **** who had fought bravely. The people loved him but many senators (important politicians in Rome) did not. Therefore, on **** March (**BC) a group of angry ******** – including Caesar's friend ****** – assassinated ****** by reportedly stabbing him over 23 times!

After his death, civil war sparked again but Caesar's nephew, ********, eventually became the first Emperor of ****, ending *** years of the Republic. From then on, the Roman Empire expanded and became even more powerful.

Although Julius Caesar stopped at nothing to reach his goals, one cannot argue that he was a remarkable man, who conquered lands and became leader of the most powerful region of the time: The Roman ******.

"Why is there some information missing, you canister of creeping cockroaches?" moaned the professor. "I didn't understand a word of that... apart from the bit about him being ruthless – just like me."

"I'm sorry. My circuits are still mending themselves after our last time adventure," Clank explained. "Perhaps we could have a day off to recover?"

"RECOVER? I don't need to recover! We will continue to plunder the hallways of time until my mission is complete. If you need a break, I can always find another robot assistant and you can join the rest of your 'friends' in the servant scrap heap? It will be the biggest 'break' you've ever had."

"No, no," responded Clank. "I don't need a break, master."

"Then let the plundering begin!"

And with that – and the final flick of a switch – both Clank and the professor vanished, leaving a silent room, awaiting the next person for Professor Plunder's collection.

CHAPTER 2:
The Snags of Time Travel

Travelling in a time machine is not for the faint hearted. Have you ever been in a fast-moving car? Your stomach jumps, you sweat nervously, the palms of your hands grow sticky and you have a slight feeling of impending DOOM (especially if you're not driving). Well, imagine travelling 100,000 times faster than the fastest car; that's what it's like to time travel.

As soon as the machine vanished from the professor's lair, they were plunged into darkness, and shot into an endless vacuum. The skin on Professor Plunder's face (which already hung like a rubber hammock from his wrinkly chin and neck) flew backwards and wrapped around the back of his head. His body shook viciously, and his bones vibrated; the attached muscles expanding then collapsing like air in a bagpipe. Without his special glasses, his eyes would have squashed into the back of his skull rendering him blind. Instead, the professor could witness time passing him by. Occasionally, he would glimpse images of important events in history (like Polaroid pictures in a scrapbook) from people celebrating the end of World War II to the invention of the first aeroplane. A glint of joy would appear in his eyes when a tyrant or dictator flicked past; he so wanted to follow in their footsteps.

Clank, on the other hand, who did not have a seatbelt or a special chair, had almost completely broken apart. His nuts and bolts had all come undone and the top of his head had crashed into the side of the machine. His circuit boards flew wildly around the capsule and his wheels bounced off the walls. Unsurprisingly, Clank did not enjoy time travel!

As they reached the end of their time journey, a small purple wormhole could be seen in front of them. Soon, this grew larger until a haze of smoke filled the landscape. At this point, the machine slowed down and all of Clank's parts came crashing to the floor.

"Clank! Why are you so noisy?" bellowed Professor Plunder. Of course, Clank could not answer because he was spewed all over the floor of the time machine.

CHAPTER 3:
An Unwanted Passenger

Fortunately for Clank (or unfortunately depending on your point of view) this humiliating exercise had happened before. The professor pressed another button on his suit and the pair of mechanical arms shot out from the ceiling. They grabbed bits of Clank and began fixing him back together; in no time Clank was repaired (but still looking a bit dishevelled!)

Professor Plunder was unbuckled by the mechanical arms and stretched triumphantly. Blue skies surrounded them and warm sunlight tickled the professor's face. They were stood on top of a hill, which was covered in lush grass. Sheep busily nibbled at the ground around them and birds chirped cheerfully in a large gnarled olive tree. In the distance, a river meandered through the green fields before the landscape began to change. An impressive ancient city could be seen across the horizon.

"Rome," Professor Plunder boasted. "The greatest city, governed by the greatest leaders. About to meet the greatest human mind in history... ME!"

As the professor continued to brag and lavish praise on himself, a soft knocking sound could be heard from within the time machine. Soon the soft knock turned into a THUMP, THUMP, THUMP!

"Clank! What is that incessant noise. Turn it off immediately!"

Clank creakily wheeled himself towards the noise, which came from a small cupboard in the corner of the machine. As he approached, he heard:

"Hey! Let me out of this thing! I think I'm going to be —"

Clank opened the cupboard.

"— SICK."

A girl in green trousers and orange t-shirt sprang out, sending vomit flying across the sides of the time machine. This triggered the sprinkler system, which soaked Clank and the girl. Another mechanical arm shot out, carrying a dripping sponge and began scrubbing. In next to no time, the machine was spotless. A second arm flew out holding a hair-dryer, which focused its efforts on Clank and the girl. Clank, in particular, was starting to short-circuit again, sending sparks flying around the machine.

By the time they were finished, Clank was almost back to normal and the girl stood there – clean and dry – with her brown hair puffed up like a toilet brush.

"What on Earth are you doing here?" bellowed Professor Plunder. "I told you to stay in your room!"

The professor clearly knew this little stowaway…

CHAPTER 4:
Meet Ava

After several minutes of the professor blabbering on…

Bla bla bla irresponsible thing to do;

Bla bla bla young people have no respect nowadays;

Bla bla bla I should never have agreed to let you stay with me;

Bla bla bla If you were my child, I'd show you what's for;

Bla bla bla you've already ruined my day;

Bla bla bla I should just leave you here to fend for yourself;

…the girl was finally allowed to speak.

"But Uncle *Basil?* – " (yes, this was Professor Plunder's real name. I think it's a lovely name but it doesn't scream 'super villain'!)

"– That is not my name. I have not used it for twenty years! You will address me as 'Professor Plunder' only."

"'Plunder?' What does that mean?" the girl asked innocently.

"It means I take whatever I want from people and cause fear and chaos where ever I go."

"Well, that doesn't sound very nice. I thought you were my squidgy uncle." Her lip began to quiver and her eyes started to fill with tears.

"No! Stop it. I can't stand crying children."

By this time, she began to wail uncontrollably. Her mouth flung wide open like a pelican's bill. Her arms flailed around and her face grew bright purple.

"Alright, alright. Call me what you like. Just stop crying."

The girl, whose name was Ava, stopped immediately, smiled sweetly and said: "Thank you uncley wunkley woo wa."

The look on Professor Plunder's face made it clear that he was not happy with his new 'pet name'.

Ava was his great niece (his sister's granddaughter in case you are scratching your head wondering what a 'great niece' is) and, since her arrival at his evil factory two days ago, she had made his life a misery. Ava was everything the professor despised about the human race: fun, sensitive, silly, smiley, sweet – yuck! So when she pestered him with 'Uncley wunkley, could I possibly have a book to read?' or 'Can I play with your robot please uncle dearest?' he felt physically sick and exhausted all at the same time.

Unfortunately for him, the professor's sister (Ava's grandmother, whose name was Ulga) was an unstoppable force, even more relentless than the professor himself. A colossal woman and former professional wrestler, she doted upon Ava. Once in a while Ulga would demand that Professor Plunder looked after Ava in order for her to have a reunion with her old wrestling buddies or for her to go on a 'wrestling cruise' somewhere in the Atlantic. She would leave strict instructions:

1) BE NICE.

2) DO NOT TORTURE OR TORMENT AVA.

3) IF YOU FAIL EITHER OF THE FIRST TWO INSTRUCTIONS, I WILL TWIST OFF YOUR SWEATY LITTLE HEAD AND FRY UP YOUR PEA-BRAIN FOR BREAKFAST.

Although he would never admit it, the professor was frightened of his sister and simply had no choice but to take Ava in.

Poor Ava's parents abandoned her when she was just a baby, so she had no other family to speak of. Of course, this didn't make the professor any kinder towards her; she was just a bogie at the end of his nose that needed flicking away, as far as he was concerned. But Ava was a lot more than 'just a bogie'. Look at these two lists:

WHAT PROFESSOR PLUNDER THINKS OF AVA:

• SHE IS ANNOYING AND STUPID.

WHAT AVA IS REALLY LIKE (THE FACTS):

• AVA IS THE TOP PUPIL IN HER CLASS. SHE IS 9 YEARS OLD BUT HAS A READING AGE OF 15. SHE LOVES BOOKS AND IS CURRENTLY READING 'WAR AND PEACE' BY LEO TOLSTOY, WHICH IS THE SIZE OF HER HEAD, HAS VERY SMALL WRITING AND ABSOLUTELY NO PICTURES! NOT STUPID AT ALL.

WHAT PROFESSOR PLUNDER THINKS OF AVA:

- SHE IS UNBEARABLY LOUD AND SCREECHY

WHAT AVA IS REALLY LIKE (THE FACTS):

- AVA IS ONLY LOUD AND SCREECHY WHEN SHE WANTS TO STOP PROFESSOR PLUNDER YELLING AT HER. THE REST OF THE TIME SHE IS QUIET AND THOUGHTFUL -- NOT THAT THE PROFESSOR WOULD NOTICE THIS!

WHAT PROFESSOR PLUNDER THINKS OF AVA:

- SHE SMELLS DISGUSTING

WHAT AVA IS REALLY LIKE (THE FACTS):

- AVA WASHES AT LEAST ONCE EVERY DAY. SHE USES A SHAMPOO THAT SMELLS OF WATERMELON. TO MOST PEOPLE, SHE SMELLS 'MEADOW FRESH' BUT NOT TO THE PROFESSOR.

WHAT PROFESSOR PLUNDER THINKS OF AVA:

- SHE IS A USELESS GIRL -- THE WORST KIND OF USELESS!

WHAT AVA IS REALLY LIKE (THE FACTS):

- AVA IS CERTAINLY NOT 'USELESS'. SHE IS A SCOUT, A COMPUTER WHIZ, A SKILLED GYMNAST AND SHE IS FANTASTIC AT FIXING BROKEN BITS AROUND HER HOUSE. SHE CAN DO EVERYTHING MOST BOYS CAN DO AND MORE.

WHAT PROFESSOR PLUNDER THINKS OF AVA:

- SHE IS TALENTLESS

WHAT AVA IS REALLY LIKE (THE FACTS):

- AVA HAS MANY TALENTS. FOR INSTANCE, SHE WON HER SCHOOL CHESS COMPETITION LAST YEAR AND CAN STAND ON HER HEAD FOR OVER TEN MINUTES. THE FACT THAT SHE CAN FOOL THE PROFESSOR INTO THINKING THAT SHE IS A PATHETIC LITTLE GIRL IS PROBABLY HER BEST TALENT. SHE ALWAYS 'PLAYS THIS ROLE' WHEN HER UNCLE LOOKS PARTICULARLY ANGRY.

WHAT PROFESSOR PLUNDER THINKS OF AVA:

- SHE IS A WASTE OF TIME

WHAT AVA IS REALLY LIKE (THE FACTS):

- ALL OF THE ABOVE SUGGESTS THAT AVA IS NOT A WASTE OF TIME. PERHAPS THE PROFESSOR SHOULD SPEND MORE TIME IN HER COMPANY -- HE MIGHT LEARN SOMETHING.

WHAT PROFESSOR PLUNDER THINKS OF AVA:

- SHE IS EXPENSIVE

WHAT AVA IS REALLY LIKE (THE FACTS):

- AVA IS NOT EXPENSIVE TO HAVE TO STAY. SHE BRINGS HER OWN FOOD (BECAUSE THE PROFESSOR'S FOOD IS DISGUSTING) AND NEVER ASKS THE PROFESSOR FOR ANY TOYS OR ICE CREAM OR ANYTHING ELSE THAT A CHILD VISITING MIGHT ASK FOR. IN FACT, HER UNCLE HAS NEVER SPENT A PENNY ON HER.

Right… back to the story!

CHAPTER 5:
Dressing Up for the Occasion

After a lot of huffing and sighing from Professor Plunder, he finally made his decision.

"You will stay here with my time machine. Hide away. Do nothing. Say nothing. You will not ruin my perfectly planned out mission –"

"– you only decided to come here this morning professor. We haven't made a plan yet," interrupted Clank honestly.

"Silence! I do not tell idiot robots about my brilliant plans," retorted the blushing professor.

"But I could help you Uncley Poo. I've read lots of books about Ancient Rome – it's one of my favourite subjects," Ava suggested.

"Silly made-up picture books are of no use to us. No, you stay here. That is final. Go and sit over there and touch nothing."

A fold-away stool flapped out from the side of the time machine. The disappointment on Ava's face was clear but there was no arguing with her stubborn uncle. She plonked herself down and folded her arms.

"Right Clank. We need to dress for Rome. I want to look stylish, handsome and dangerous! What are my options?"

The projector beamed out of Clank's stomach again, this time showing a 3D wardrobe with a selection of different clothing styles for the professor to browse.

"I would recommend this one," advised Clank. He highlighted a majestic, long white toga and gold wreath for his head. "This is what all the important Romans used to wear."

"Yuck! A dress! I'm not wearing that. I want to look brave,

courageous, strong. That one looks more like it."

The professor pointed to a rather skimpy looking outfit. It was mostly made from leather but had extra metal padding on the waistband and shoulders. There were leather pads around the arms and wrists, and shin protection made from animal skin on the legs, as well as some long sandals. Apart from that, there was nothing on the chest and only a loin cloth (or big pants!) to stop him from being completely naked! 'Why would the professor choose this outfit?' you may ask. Well, for one huge reason: The enormous, shiny, vicious-looking sword that came with it.

"Yes, yes. Everyone will fear me if I wear that outfit. I will use the sword to slay anyone who gets in my way. Ya, take that, ya, and that!" This was the noise of the professor pretending to butcher his enemies with an invisible sword. (It looked more like he was swinging a wet, lifeless fish!)

"But professor –" Clank interrupted.

"– no buts, no ifs Clank. I've made up my mind. Get me dressed and we'll begin our mission."

Clank rolled his metal eyeballs. He knew there was no persuading the professor to change his mind. It was going to be a long day! The professor had chosen to dress like a gladiator, the fearsome fighting men of Rome. Clank had a bad feeling that this could cause them trouble. However, Clank did as he was told (as usual) and pressed a button on the side of the time machine, whilst the professor stepped back inside. The mechanical arms came back out and proceeded to undress the professor (Ava closed her eyes for this bit!) He was then dressed in his chosen outfit. When they were finished, the arms disappeared and the professor stepped out, puffing his chest like a heroic warrior.

This was what he actually looked like:

"Now I look deadly and dashing, get yourself dressed Clank. Typical servant wear will suffice. Hurry up," ordered the professor.

"Can I have a costume?" asked Ava, jumping up from her seat.

"Absolutely not. You are staying here, hiding away. We are not playing dress up little girl. This is serious business." He said all of this whilst staring at himself in a mirror that had popped out of the time machine. He was twirling and posing like a catwalk model.

Ava looked hurt and slumped down on the stool again, this time with her head in her hands. The professor ignored her and began walking in the direction of the city.

Before she had the chance to feel sorry for herself, Ava felt a little prod in her back. It was Clank, who was now kitted out in a red tunic that covered his whole robotic body, hiding his mechanical under-carriage. He had a mask over his face which made him look surprisingly human and a laurel wreath upon his head; the perfect Roman disguise – for a robot, at least!

Clank whispered: "Your outfit is in the time machine." He winked and smiled before chasing after Professor Plunder, who was shouting:

"CLANK! COME ON! WE HAVEN'T GOT ALL DAY!"

Ava leapt up and skipped into the machine, dressing herself quickly in a white tunic and long green cloak. Perhaps she was going to see Ancient Rome after all.

CHAPTER 6:
Roman Around

"Keep up Clank. I have other business to attend to today. No time to dawdle!" The professor was surprisingly quick on his feet for an older man with a peg leg, especially if he had some plundering to do.

"Where is Julius Caesar right now? We need to snatch him and take him back before the end of the day."

"I'm not too sure, Professor sir," Clank mumbled nervously. "My circuits are still recovering from the journey. What I can tell you is that he enjoyed watching a good fight to the death so perhaps we could head towards the Colosseum?"

"That's another thing we have in common – I love a good fight to the death too. We're going to get along famously! Lead on, you old rust bucket."

"I'll do my best sir professor sir. My historical GPS seems to be in working order. I think it's this way." He pointed over a bridge, and towards the main city. Suddenly the countryside and winding river had transformed into a bustling city. A huge stone structure, with soaring arches seemed to wrap around and through the city.

"That's a Roman aqueduct," explained Clank excitedly. "The Romans used them to transport fresh water into their cities."

"Why didn't they just use a tap like the rest of us? Honestly, these primitive people don't have any common sense," Professor Plunder interrupted.

Feeling a little frustrated by the professor's lack of respect and knowledge, Clank bit his electronic tongue and said, "They did have taps in Roman times your professorship sir. In fact, the Ancient Romans were very good plumbers. The water for the taps had to come from somewhere and that was the job of the aqueducts."

"Basic brutes the lot of them!"

The professor had stopped listening, so Clank just followed on in silence. They continued walking along a dead straight paved road, through streets of white-walled houses with red tiled roofs. Large green spaces with flowing fountains were all around them and the sheer size and elegance of some of the buildings was sending Clank's bolts into a spin. Even the professor remarked on the many crystal-white marble statues.

"I want ten of those in my first palace after I take over the world. All in my image with rippling muscles and chiselled, handsome face." Clank looked down towards the professor's big belly then up towards his scarred, bearded face. He wondered whether the professor was looking at a different reflection of himself in the mirror every morning.

"Next left," instructed Clank. They moved around the corner to find a very different part of Ancient Rome. Multi-storey houses were crammed together and the alleyways were narrow and dark. People buzzed around everywhere, pushing into Clank and the professor as they went about their working days. Market stalls were scattered around selling all sorts of Roman delicacies; from baskets loaded with fruit and barrels filled with wine to stalls selling pottery and others offering live animals for sale. The professor held his hand to his nose – the smell of animal droppings, fresh sewage and fish guts was turning his stomach.

"This doesn't look much like the Colosseum, Clank. Are we lost again, you enormous brainless dustbin?"

"I'm sorry your majesty professor sir. Maybe my historical GPS needs a re-boot. I'll do it now." Clank stopped in the middle of the street and flicked a switch on the side of his head. This seemed to completely turn him off for a few seconds before he started to shake, twirl around on the spot then play a welcome message: "Introducing the newest Clank model. A robot servant for all your evil needs."

"Have you quite finished?" moaned Professor Plunder.

"Ah, yes. That feels better. My systems are back in working order. Oh… we're on the wrong side of the city. Oops!"

The professor's fist came hurtling down on top of Clank's head. "A robot servant for all my needs? More like jelly-brained nuisance!"

All of a sudden, the professor felt a scratch on the side of his leg. It was his sword being whisked away from its scabbard. He looked down to see a dirty little face staring up at him; a young boy, who smiled before stamping on the professor's only foot and scampering away up one of the alleyways.

"Oi you! That's my sword!" yelled the professor as he chased after the boy, closely followed by Clank, who rattled as he ran.

They trailed the boy through backstreets, over sacks of grain, down cobbled steps and under wooden carts. The professor was surprisingly nimble for his age and size – he lived for moments when he could chase down his prey – and soon he was only inches away from the thief. He rustled around in a pouch on the side of his gladiator outfit and grabbed a gun-shaped object which had the words 'Plunder Buster' written on the side in red. Still chasing the boy, he twisted the Plunder Buster to the 'lasso' setting, pointed it at the boy and fired. A length of rope snaked out of the end of the gadget, which twisted around the boy's legs causing him to trip and fall flat on his face. By now, they had chased into an open space. Manicured gardens and clipped hedges were surrounded by immense temples and government buildings.

As the professor reached down to grab his sword from the boy and place it back in its sheath, he was interrupted by a booming, imposing voice:

"You there. Gladiator. What are you doing out in the city? You are a prisoner of Rome!" Two Roman soldiers stood in front of them.

The shocked little boy wriggled out of the rope around his ankles and sprinted away into the darkness of an alleyway, dropping the sword in the process. Clank, who had struggled to keep up, came crashing into one of the soldiers. Soon, he was being held in the air by his collar and the professor was handcuffed and chained up.

"Think you can escape the Colosseum do you? Well, we'll see how you like a meeting with the 'Savage Beast'!" Both of the soldiers laughed ominously and pushed Clank and the professor onwards.

'The Savage Beast'? Neither Clank or the professor liked the sound of that. They gulped and trudged forward. Was this the end of Professor Plunder's attempt to take over the world?

In the shadows, the silhouette of a small girl could be seen – Ava. She was now their only hope.

CHAPTER 7:
Ava's Plan

Ava had been following her uncle from afar. Never letting Clank and the professor out of her sight. She knew that she would get into trouble for disobeying her uncle but wanted so much to glimpse Rome in all its glory. Ava was also curious to see what her uncle was up to – she suspected it was nothing good. Luckily, she had witnessed the boy steal the professor's sword and kept up with them as they chased through the streets of Ancient Rome. She had even seen where the boy who stole the sword had come from: a small house just off the main street. This is where she decided to return.

After hanging around for a while in a passageway to the side of the house, Ava witnessed a kind-looking lady cradling a baby, humming and smiling as she tried to send the tiny bundle to sleep. Soon after, the boy came running towards the lady with the baby and they shared a loving embrace. He was thin and had a hang-dog look about him. Ava felt sorry for him; clearly, he was trying to steal the sword to support and provide for his family.

Ava waited for a time when the lady returned indoors and the boy was sat on the doorstep, on his own, before approaching him.

"Salve," said Ava *(this means 'hello' in Latin; the language that the Romans spoke. She was pretty much fluent, having taught herself Latin last summer when she was trapped in her bedroom whilst staying with the professor. I'll translate the rest of the conversation into English – after all, I'm not as clever as Ava; not many people are!)*

"Hello," replied the boy.

"My name is Ava. What's yours?"

"I'm Darius. What do you want?" Darius seemed tired and his eyes were red, as though he had been crying.

"You look hungry," suggested Ava. "Will you help me if I promise to provide food for you and your family?"

"How can you do that?" asked Darius sceptically.

"I saw you try to steal that sword —"

Darius rose up hastily, looking for somewhere to escape.

"Please. I'm not going to hurt you and I won't tell the soldiers it was you." Still suspicious, Darius nodded for Ava to continue. "I know how to get you that sword. You could sell it and eat well for a year."

"I know that! I nearly had it, but that man used his sorcery on me."

"That wasn't sorcery. It was technology," explained Ava.

Darius looked perplexed.

"That man is my uncle," Ava continued. "I know where he is and he will give you his sword… if you help him to escape."

"Escape?" cried Darius. "Where does he need to escape from?"

"The Colosseum," answered Ava. There was a moment of

stunned silence. "Those soldiers took them there. I'm sure there must be a way to get in."

Darius fixed Ava with a serious glare. "There is a way in. But it won't be easy. The Colosseum is designed to keep prisoners in, but they're not so worried about keeping the public out. Follow me." With that, Darius took Ava's hand and they sprinted off down another dark alley in the direction of the Colosseum.

CHAPTER 8:
The Beast Awaits

Meanwhile, the professor and Clank had been escorted to a dark, grimy cell beneath the Colosseum. Two tough looking Roman soldiers stood guard at the entrance and several other men lay about the room, awaiting their fate in the arena above. They could hear clashes of steel upon steel, grunts of effort from the competitors and roars of appreciation from the hungry crowd. Clank stood shaking in the corner of the cell as a rat crawled over his head.

"My data tells me that there is no way of escaping this cell, Professor sir. We are doomed to a warrior's death in the great arena!" Clank whimpered.

"Oh, stop your whinging you bag of bolts!" pleaded Professor Plunder. "It is not my destiny to die here. I have too many evil deeds to perform. I will battle my way out and fight off anyone who stands in my way."

Somehow this did not comfort Clank, who began leaking oily tears from his eye sockets. He had seen the professor trying to 'fight' over the years. This usually ended with him commanding one of his robot soldiers to sort out his skirmishes for him; a luxury they didn't have with them today. The professor was also old, weak and unreasonably over-confident – a recipe for disaster!

"Stop crying and give me some information about the beasts we're likely to encounter."

"Of course, your professorness. Here it is…"

Romans loved a spectacle and there was nothing more spectacular than watching a crazed wild animal in the arena. Exotic animals such as leopards, lions, tigers, elephants, bears and even crocodiles were used to entertain the crowds. Sometimes they were captured by skilled huntsmen for entertainment and at other times they were made to fight prisoners. Such animal combat was saved for the lowest criminals as a form of execution.

"Hang on a minute!" interrupted Professor Plunder. "Lowest form of criminals? Who do they think they are? I am no low criminal – I am a criminal mastermind!"

"Might I finish, your majesty professor sir?" asked Clank.

"Go on then," replied the professor, who was now in an even worse mood.

Most animals were slaughtered in the arena, although some (like zebras and ostriches) were used to pull chariots.

Julius Caesar particularly enjoyed using lions in the Colosseum because they demonstrated his power and strength but glorious battles involving elephants, in particular, were also staged. The animal were kept hungry to make them even more desperate and blood-thirsty. There was nothing a Roman crowd liked better than to see someone torn limb from limb by a rabid, ravenous, savage beast.

"Alright. I get the point. You can stop going on about this hopeless situation," grumbled the professor. "I was expecting you to come up with some useful information, not that depressing rubbish! So, it's a herd of elephants to trample all over us or a drooling, starving lion to rip us to pieces. Just brilliant!"

He slumped on to the floor, head in his hands.

Meanwhile, in the corner of their cell, a man the size of a small truck sat staring at the grubby stone floor. His muscles bulged out of his tunic and his rough, beaten face suggested he was a seasoned fighter. The scars on his body were proof of his many victories in the arena.

One of the guards opened the barred gate, shouting: "Prisoner number 1 for the Savage Beast!"

The enormous man crumpled to the ground, begging for mercy: "Please, please. Not the Savage Beast. Anything but that!" Several more guards marched in, grabbed the man on all sides and pulled him – kicking and screaming – out of the cell. The gate clattered closed leaving a hushed, shocked silence. Moments later, the man's cries could be heard overhead. These were followed by a brutal, thunderous roar and the loudest, gut-churning scream Clank had ever heard. Even the professor gulped at this sound.

Enthusiastic cheers told them that the fight had lasted less than ten seconds and that the enormous, muscular man was now dead at the hands (or claws) of the Savage Beast.

The gates opened one more time. "Prisoners number 2 and 3" were called. It was Clank and Professor Plunder's turn. Before they had a chance to run, they were seized by some burly guards and carried out of the gate and up a dimly-lit corridor to a set of heavy wooden doors. Through a crack in the doors, Clank could see a packed arena, with people clapping eagerly for new victims to face the Savage Beast. The stench of rotting flesh and stale blood cut through the air and both the professor and Clank felt sweat drip down their foreheads. In Clank's case, this was beads of condensed steam as his system overheated with fear. He turned to the professor, who was now trembling, and took his hand. For once, Professor Plunder didn't refuse Clank's show of kindness and as the doors flung open, they stepped into the Colosseum hand in hand to await their horrific fates.

CHAPTER 9:
Fighting for Their Lives

The brightness of the sun stung the professor's eyes. He glanced up at the stands towering above him; and all around him were people baying for blood and shouting for the Savage Beast to rip them apart. The sand-covered arena was currently empty, as bodies from previous victims had been scooped up and taken away on carts. Suddenly, Clank's circuit boards began to tickle as his eye socket zoomed into a raised area on the first level of spectators. He saw a richly decorated chair, on top of a podium and a grandly-dressed man sitting on it.

"I've found Julius Caesar!" exclaimed Clank.

"What? Where?" demanded the professor.

Clank pointed up to the platform. They both watched as Julius Caesar stood up, waved to his adoring public and left the amphitheatre through an archway, into a tunnel.

"He's getting away Clank. You are not helping my mood," moaned Professor Plunder. "We have to follow him… anyway, why is he leaving before he sees us fight. That's terribly disrespectful!"

"I don't know. My data still has some gaps after all the time travelling we've been doing. Perhaps he's got better things to do than to watch an old professor and a glitchy robot get eaten alive."

The professor slapped Clank on the side of the head. "Old?! I am not old! You cheeky –"

His rant was interrupted by the entrance of a gigantic, black-maned lion into the arena. Professor Plunder and

Clank stood open-mouthed as the Savage Beast, with teeth like piercing daggers and claws like thick razors, began to stalk its prey. The lion's eyes were dark and haunted but fully focused on the professor and Clank. In the blink of an eye, the Savage Beast, sprinted viciously towards them, drool spilling from its hungry jaws.

"Split up!" Clank yelled to the professor, who was frozen to the spot, holding his gladiator's sword as effectively as a limp banana.

As though it were a coiled spring, the lion leapt into the air.

Snapping out of his fearful trance, Professor Plunder rolled creakily out of the way, just inches from the beast's grasp. He then began to run along the edge of the arena, whilst Clank scooted the other way. The crowd booed and howled at this momentary escape, but the lion reset itself for another attack.

"Psssst!" The professor heard a sound coming from the floor of the arena and looked around to see a metal grate leading to the sewage tunnels underneath the Colosseum. On the other side of the grate was his niece, Ava.

"You can get out this way, uncle," whispered Ava as loudly as she could without drawing attention.

"I thought I told you to stay with the time machine!" barked the professor. "I have this situation completely under control, thank you." He said this as the Savage Beast sprung once more, headbutting the professor and sending flying up in the air.

"Alright. We'll leave you to it then," shouted Ava sarcastically with Professor Plunder rolling around painfully in the sand.

"No, no!" Clank interjected. "Stay there. I think we can get away... Professor sir, set your Plunder Buster to 'freeze' then point it at the Beast. It won't give us much time but, if Ava

41

can open the grate, we may be able to escape."

"That's just what I was going to do you carton of clotted cream! You don't need to tell me what the plan is!"

In actual fact, with all the panic of fighting the Savage Beast, the professor had completely forgotten about his special weapon and was deeply relieved to fumble around for it under his Roman costume. With no time to lose – and with the lion about to open his gaping jaws and swallow the professor's head – he aimed the Plunder Buster. A bright blue ray shot out, capturing the Savage Beast in a frozen bubble. The professor then twisted a mechanism on the side of his weapon to 'FULL POWER' and pointed it at the angry crowd. Immediately, a bright blue beam spread throughout the Colosseum, capturing the entire audience in a frozen forcefield.

"We've got ten seconds!" yelled Clank.

They both raced for their lives and slid towards the now opened grate, disappearing just in time for the stunned crowd and confused beast to wake from their trance. The two 'gladiators' in the arena had disappeared, as though they had vanished into thin air. A bemused silence spread across the Colosseum; perhaps the beast had swallowed them both whole? The incident was soon forgotten when the next poor victim was pushed into the arena and the 'sport' could continue. The crowd began to yell and clap again and, once more, the Savage Beast stalked its prey.

CHAPTER 10:
Underground Arguments

"Phew, I thought we were cat food there," said Clank, looking thankfully over to Ava and noticing another shadow in the darkness.

"You!" bellowed Professor Plunder. "You tried to steal my sword you little thief!"

In case you've forgotten, Ava entrusted a Roman boy, Darius, to help her to rescue her uncle and Clank.

"Shh!" interjected Ava. "We're not safe yet. The guards are still looking for us. This is Darius. He guided me through this sewer network so that I could help you escape. He is my friend. Please be kind to him."

"Kind? Kind!" the professor shrieked, but whispered at the same time. "I'm in this mess *because* of him. I wouldn't have been caught chasing around the streets of Rome if it wasn't for him."

"The reason you were caught is because you chose to wear that ridiculous gladiator outfit. You were bound to be caught at some point today. Gladiators were slaves and prisoners in the eyes of Ancient Rome. They wouldn't have just wandered around the city doing their shopping," argued Ava, sticking up for her friend and challenging her uncle for the first time in her life."

"Well, I —"

"— and speaking of that costume, put this on. You'll blend in better."

Ava passed over a red tunic, which the professor reluctantly put on, replacing the leather-clad gladiator clothes. He now looked like any other Roman citizen, which of course put him in a bad mood.

"What is that hideous stench?" the professor quickly changed the subject.

"It's probably pee and poo," Clank interrupted helpfully. "The Romans built sewers underneath the city to get rid of their waste. Just think, we could be wading through Julius Caesar's urine right now!"

"Oh, what a novel and completely revolting thought," grumbled the professor, who was used to the finer things in life; not treading around in human waste and getting it caught in between his toes. "How do we get out of this wretched place before I vomit?"

'There's probably some vomit in here too actually," began Clank...

With this, Professor Plunder gagged before spewing up his dinner from the night before.

"Darius will help us navigate the tunnels and return back to the time machine," said Ava, with a supportive hand on Darius' shoulder. "He knows them like the back of his hand."

"What a skill to have. Just shows what a sewer rat he is!" the professor sneered before vomiting some more.

"I would be a bit nicer to Darius if I were you, or we'll be stuck in these tunnels for a lot longer," reasoned Ava.

"I am Professor Plunder: Conqueror of the world! I am not nice to thieves and gutter rats. Anyway, what's in it for him? Why is he helping me?"

Suddenly Ava looked a bit sheepish.

"I may have possibly told him he could... have your sword."

"My sword?! My sword! What does he want with this priceless, one-of-a-kind blade? Made from deepest volcanic platinum in the mines of Mount Doom. Many slaves met their peril producing this weapon of superior quality. The hilt is encrusted with rare Amazonian diamonds and the pommel is layered with eighty-seven carat gold. A slave boy could not possibly wield such a foil of engineering genius." The professor looked extremely pleased with his (made-up) speech.

After a period of silence, Clank couldn't help himself: "Umm... actually. I picked it up on the internet. It's just a replica sword. Not worth a great deal and I'm pretty sure it was produced in a factory somewhere in Hull; not in the deepest mines of Mount Doom."

This was swiftly followed by a clanging kick to his bottom from Professor Plunder.

"You see!" began Ava. "The sword is not worth a great deal to us but to Darius, he could sell it and help to feed his family. I met them and they're very poor. His baby sister needs some fresh milk and his mother hasn't eaten for days."

"Save the sob stories. I'm not in the mood. ALRIGHT. He

can have the stupid sword – I never liked it anyway – as soon as he gets us out of here. But I'm not ready to go back to the time machine empty-handed. He must take us to Julius Caesar or it's no deal."

"Why do you need to be taken to Julius Caesar? What do you mean 'empty-handed'?" asked Ava suspiciously. She knew that her uncle was up to something but wasn't aware of Professor Plunder's actual evil intentions.

The professor paused, contemplating his reply. "He just has something I want... a souvenir if you like. I don't like to use my time machine and not bring something special back, that's all," he lied unconvincingly. "Tell the boy to take us to him." He smiled, which made him look even more creepy and untrustworthy.

Ava tentatively translated this to Darius, who nodded but shrugged at the same time, mumbling something to Ava in Latin.

"What's the peasant saying?" demanded the professor.

"He says that he will take you to Julius Caesar but that he doesn't know where he is."

"Useless cretin! Clank – where is the man?"

"I think he's heading for the Theatre of Pompey. Not sure why – probably to make a speech or something," said Clank, who still wasn't receiving all the information he needed.

"Hang on a minute! What is today's date?" asked Ava urgently.

"It's 15th March, 44BC," answered Clank.

"Oh no! Don't you know what happens today?"

They all looked blank.

"Julius Caesar is assassinated on the Ides of March."

Still blank.

"Today! He's going to be stabbed to death by members of the senate… and it all happens in the Theatre of Pompey."

Stunned, the professor began to panic. "Right little slave boy. Take us to the Theatre of Pompey and the sword is yours. He had better not be dead by the time we get there or the deal's off."

Darius had a look of determination in his eyes before splashing off up one of the tunnels, with Ava, Clank and the professor following closely behind.

CHAPTER 11:
Seizing Caesar

After a few minutes of trudging through the underground tunnel system (and trying to avoid puddles of Roman toilet waste!) Darius at last guided the group to a ladder and a chink of light above them pointed to an exit from the sewer. They climbed up the ladder which took them to another narrow street and they followed Darius until they reached some steps that led to a huge doorway into a grand building. With real urgency, the Professor wrestled through the crowds in front of him (all clearly wanting to get a glimpse of their leader) elbowing himself into a sloped auditorium; much like the Colosseum but smaller and more ornately decorated. Red and grey pillars adorned the auditorium, whilst hundreds of archways encircled the beautiful structure.

"Caesar is just over there!" shouted Clank, who was using his built-in binoculars. He pointed to a gathering of men wearing stylish white togas striped with purple, who were disappearing through an archway.

"Quickly, you fools!" babbled the professor. "We're losing them."

Professor Plunder felt a firm tug on his own toga and looked down to see Darius, who was sporting a dogged expression. Darius pointed to the Professor's belt, demanding something of him in Latin.

"He wants the sword now," interpreted Ava. "He says he has taken you to Caesar and done all that you asked."

"And now he is wasting my time and stopping me from stealing Caesar!" blurted out Professor Plunder, who immediately realised what he had said.

"Stealing him?!" exclaimed Ava. "I knew you were up to something. You can't parade around time stealing famous people. Messing about with time is totally immoral!"

"Oh, save your stupid moral compass! I knew I should have left you in the sewer." With this, the professor drew his sword and threw it towards Darius and Ava, who both had to duck out of the way, falling over each other in the process. They glanced up to see the professor fleeing towards the archway where Caesar had stood moments earlier, closely trailed by a misguidedly loyal Clank.

"How could he?" cried Ava. "No sane person would try to capture Julius Caesar in Rome and drag him back into the future. He is meddling with the hands of time. We have to stop him."

Darius nodded. He had won his prized sword but still wanted to stand by his new friend. He took Ava's hand and they sprinted after the others, not knowing if they would be too late to stop Professor Plunder…

CHAPTER 12:
Time is Ticking

The professor – with Clank shuffling around behind him trying to keep up – hurried through another archway to reveal an enormous white-marbled courtyard, which was surrounded by more archways and pillars. Bright, sweet-smelling gardens interlaced with fountains filled the space, as a mosaic path steered them towards another building, festooned in red and grey stone. The professor didn't stop to marvel at the scenery; he had one thing on his mind: to capture Caesar before his assassination.

A hundred metres ahead of them, they could see Caesar and his entourage climb a set of stairs and begin to make their way into the government building. There was no time to lose.

Like a young gazelle, the professor bounded up the stairs (three at a time) and vanished inside the building. Clank, who found stairs difficult with his rust-jointed spherical leg, moved considerably slower and he was soon overtaken by Ava and Darius.

Clank yelled ahead of them: "Don't do anything stupid. The professor is not going to like you interfering."

"I don't care," replied Ava. "What he's doing is wrong. We have to stop him."

They sprinted through the doors to see the professor taking out his Plunder Buster and pointing it at a large group of men, all grasping daggers in their hands, ready to strike. Caesar cowered in the middle of them, penned in on all sides.

"STOP RIGHT THERE!" the professor roared at the top of his voice. "Put your daggers down or you're all DOOMED!"

The crowd of men simultaneously turned on the spot. Who was this strange man speaking a strange language and what was the weapon he was holding? They looked like they were in some sort of enraged trance and, still with daggers raised, turned on the professor, who had expected them to drop their weapons and cower in fear. Panicking, he set his Plunder Buster to 'immobilise', pointing and shooting it at the angry mob. One by one, their legs froze and they fell flat on their faces like human dominoes.

Just as Professor Plunder was gaining the upper hand, two small hands grasped his weapon (this was Ava) and another set wrapped around his leg (this was Darius). Off balance and unable to aim, the professor's Plunder Buster started firing into the sky. Great swathes of the ceiling cracked and collapsed to the floor and all three of them had to dive out of the way.

While this was happening, Julius Caesar was picking himself up, confused but grateful to have escaped death. Before he had time to take a relieved breath, he turned around and was greeted by a different set of blood-thirsty eyes. It was another senator who had hidden behind the crowd of men, avoiding the Plunder Buster's rays.

"Brutus? My friend. Not you as well!"

Brutus lifted his dagger, stabbing Caesar directly in the heart. Caesar collapsed in a crumpled heap. He was dead.

"Noooo!" cried the professor. "He was mine for the taking!"

Suddenly, the room began to fill with sword-wielding, armour-clad Roman soldiers, all mobilised by the chaos heard inside the government building. Before the professor, Ava and Darius could be surrounded and arrested, a bright purple forcefield covered the entire chamber. Clank stood at the side of the room with the light beaming from his stomach. He had used his forcefield, which he only unleashed in extreme emergencies. Everyone in the building, except Professor Plunder and the children, stood frozen solid like ice sculptures.

"Quickly," beseeched Clank. "I don't have much more battery power. Get out this way." He pointed to a side exit on to the street.

They did as he asked, rushing outside, closely followed by Clank. As they travelled back through the Roman streets, a weary Clank panted: "The forcefield doesn't last for long but it's really effective. When they all un-freeze, they won't remember a thing from the previous 60 seconds. They'll just wake up to Brutus holding a bloodied knife and Caesar lying dead at his feet. They won't even know we were there."

"That's brilliant Clank. It means we haven't changed history too much – Brutus was one of Caesar's most trusted generals and being part of his assassination was the greatest act of betrayal," explained Ava. "Thank you for saving us. But how will they explain the ceiling falling in?"

"That's easy. The Romans are superstitious people; they will believe that it was divine intervention and that one of their gods was angered by Brutus' actions," Clank explained proudly.

"Oh, you've thought about everything haven't you, you big-headed metal maggot," whined the professor. "You didn't think to use that forcefield when I was winning did you!"

Clank looked embarrassed by this comment. He had actually reached the building before the ceiling fell in but chose to observe proceedings, rather than join in. It was only when he thought Ava and Darius were in trouble that he stepped in and used his emergency forcefield.

The professor turned furiously to Ava and Darius.

"If it wasn't for you two, I would have completed my plundering mission. You have ruined everything," he moaned like a spoilt child who couldn't have an ice cream. "I should Plunder Buster the both of you and get rid of you forever."

"But Uncley Wunkley," Ava began, putting on her babyish voice. "Auntie Ulga will be vewy cwoss with you if I'm not there when she comes to pick me up. She said she would pull out your intestines and fry them up for breaky-fast if you did anything nasty wasty to me." Ava smiled sweetly and batted her eyelids.

"AGGGH! Alright!" bellowed the frustrated professor. "You can come back with us but don't expect any supper you little leach!"

He turned to Darius, glared at him and yelled: "Get out of here you little sewer rat, before I change my mind," and marched off towards the time machine.

Ava stopped to hug her new friend and set off after the Professor. Darius watched them disappear around the corner, grasped his sword in both hands and turned towards home. He thought about telling his mother about what he had just seen and the unexpected adventures of his day but decided she wouldn't believe him anyway. Who had ever heard of a bright purple forcefield or a Plunder Buster? How could he tell her that he (and a friend from the future) had helped an evil professor and his robot to escape from the Colosseum and that he'd been in the Theatre of Pompey when the great Julius Caesar was assassinated?

No, he would keep this day a secret for the rest of his life and hope that his new sword would bring him better fortune.

CHAPTER 13:
Returning Home

The three time-travellers made their way back to the time machine without being followed or accosted. All the people they encountered seemed to be heading in the opposite direction – to Pompey's Theatre – as news filtered around the city that Caesar had been assassinated. There was a distinct anger in the air, after all, Caesar was the 'leader of people' and a much-admired man.

When they reached their transport, the professor grumpily pointed to the cupboard Ava had stowed away in before. With little choice, Ava reluctantly squeezed back in and braced herself for the journey back home. As it happened, the way back was a lot less awful; it turns out that travelling forwards in time is 'the right way' to go. Smooth but twice as quick, it was like the corridors of time were sending a message: 'Do not go back and meddle with past events. Looking forward and accepting your fate is the way humans should live.' That was what Ava pondered anyway, as the time machine slowed before Clank, who was surprisingly in one piece, opened up the cupboard for her with a reassuring smile.

The professor was nowhere to be seen; all Ava heard from him was an angry slam of his bedroom door.

The last week of Ava's stay in the professor's home was a quiet one. She barely saw her uncle. If she did bump into him, he would either turn in the other direction or completely ignore her existence, avoiding eye contact at all times. He would then stomp into a room that had a sign on the door saying: '**STRICTLY NO ACCESS. ESPECIALLY NO CHILDREN OR STUPID ROBOTS**'. He clearly hadn't forgiven either Ava or Clank. She could understand why the professor was cross with her but felt truly sorry for Clank, who had remained loyal throughout and had rescued them all.

Pressing her ear to the door, she could hear frantic banging and the fizzing of sparks from a welding iron. He was making something. Ava could only guess at what new dreadful invention was being created. All she knew was that her uncle was a tyrant like no other and needed to be stopped, somehow.

The final day of Ava's stay was a surprising one. She was woken by Clank, who was whistling cheerfully whilst carrying breakfast for her – piping hot pancakes and maple syrup. He was happy to see her and especially pleased to watch her polish off the whole plate; the professor rarely even touched the food Clank lovingly prepared for him.

"It's your last day here so the professor decided to send you off with a hearty breakfast," explained Clank. Ava knew what her uncle was doing. He was trying to 'butter her up' before her Aunt Ulga collected her. She was too hungry to refuse and had already decided not to tell her Aunt about the professor's ill-treatment of her. Ulga would stop her from visiting again and Ava simply had to get back to find out what the professor was scheming and, most importantly, how to stop him.

"Before you leave, I wanted to share something with you," said Clank excitedly. "Your friend Darius made quite a difference after we left. Turns out he was a decorated Centurion in the Roman Army before he became chief advisor to Octavian Caesar. Here's a picture of him."

"He's holding the sword we gave him!" cried Ava. "I'm so glad he lived such a full life."

"Look even closer. Can you see what is engraved on the sword?"

Ava drew the picture closer to her. Written on the sword were the words 'In Ava we trust' in Latin.

"Seems like you made quite an impression on him," Clank winked. "Maybe he was trying to spur you on and give you courage?"

Ava beamed then hugged Clank, who flinched a little, not expecting her affection.

After that, Clank helped Ava with her bags. At the bottom of the stairs she was greeted by her Aunt Ulga and a smiling Professor Plunder.

"There she is!" exclaimed the professor. He ruffled her hair and continued to smile; a smile that lasted far too long to be genuine.

"Hello dear Ava. I trust you've had a good time with Uncle Basil?" enquired Aunt Ulga.

Ava paused. She wanted to make the professor sweat.

Tentatively, she lied, "Yes, thank you. I had great fun. I love it here."

She looked over to the professor who now looked relieved. He had escaped a beating from his giant sister.

"That's wonderful darling," responded Ulga. "I'm glad you said that because I'm going away again on a special wrestling training camp in a few weeks' time. You can stay with your uncle again if you like. Can't she Basil?"

The professor's smile vanished. He was now going red in the face with frustration. Through gritted teeth he said, "Yes. Of course. That. Would. Be. Nice."

"Excellent. It's settled then," chuckled Ulga. "Come on Ava. Let's stop off and get ice cream on the way home." She scooped up Ava with one hand, placing her on her shoulders like she was a rag doll and they both cheerfully left the professor's lair.

Ava looked back to see a deep fury in the professor's eyes. He was clearly about to burst with anger. In a final act of defiance, she smiled and waved back at him. Ava didn't know what was in store for her on her next visit. But she did know one thing – next time she would be prepared.

ABOUT THE CREATORS

Keith Hatton

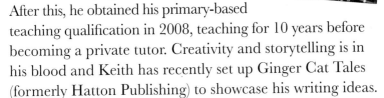

Keith is a Cambridge-based author, a teacher, a tutor and a gardener. He attended the University of East Anglia to study Drama before heading to Central School of Speech and Drama, achieving an MA in Acting Musical Theatre. After this, he obtained his primary-based teaching qualification in 2008, teaching for 10 years before becoming a private tutor. Creativity and storytelling is in his blood and Keith has recently set up Ginger Cat Tales (formerly Hatton Publishing) to showcase his writing ideas.

Keith doesn't know where the idea for Professor Plunder came from but hopes he's nothing like the mean, selfish professor. He'd like to thank all the grumpy science teachers he had when he was growing up for the inspiration.

Stewart Harris

Stewart is a Cambridge-based illustrator and graphic designer. He studied at Winchester School of Art, Chelsea College of Art and Design, and Anglia Ruskin. Being also a musician, much of his work is music-related, having designed and illustrated numerous record sleeves and gig posters.

When he's not drawing, singing or playing, Stewart enjoys cookery and wildlife – though not, he is keen to point out, at the same time.

Other books also available from Ginger Cat Tales...

Go to
www.gingercattales.com
to find out more.

If you'd like to book Keith for your school, please contact him via the Ginger Cat Tales contact page.

www.gingercattales.com